Barbie™

i can be...

A Sports Star

By Mary Man-Kong
Illustrated by Ji Young An

Random House 🏠 **New York**

Published in the United States by Random House Children's Books, a division of Random House, Inc.,
1745 Broadway, New York, NY 10019, and in Canada by Random House of Canada Limited, Toronto.
ISBN: 978-0-307-93130-6
randomhouse.com/kids   MANUFACTURED IN CHINA   10 9 8 7 6 5 4 3 2
3-D special effects and production: Red Bird Publishing Ltd., U.K.

Did you know that more than 40 million kids participate in sports in the United States? I love getting up, getting out, and getting into sports, from karate to gymnastics to soccer!

SOCCER

I love soccer! It's the most popular sport in the world. Soccer is all about teamwork—and you really need to use your head!

KARATE

Karate is a martial art that started in Japan. It's great for keeping a focused mind and body. One of the most powerful moves in karate is the roundhouse kick. *Kiai!*

ICE-SKATING

I've been ice-skating since I was Chelsea's age. It takes hours of practice, but practice makes perfect. I learned the figure eight, then advanced to the axel—and now I can even do a camel spin!

GYMNASTICS

Nikki and I both signed up for gymnastics when we were five years old. Gymnastics requires agility, strength, flexibility, coordination, and balance—and it's one of the most graceful sports!

SWIMMING

Did you know that swimming works out all of your body's major muscles? I've been swimming since I was a little girl, and now I swim like a mermaid!

SNOWBOARDING

I love to surf and I love to ski—and snowboarding is a combination of the two! Nothing is better than getting some air underneath me as I do ollies, wildcats, and alley-oops!

TENNIS

Did you know that the first women to play in the Wimbledon tournament wore full-length dresses? Thank goodness fashion has changed with the times! I have a mean serve, and I think tennis is aces!

BASKETBALL

Basketball is a real team sport. Our team practices every day, and it's all about working together. I always pass the ball to Summer so she can go for a three-pointer!

BASEBALL

I may be the pitcher of my high school baseball team, but I love hitting, too. Hey, batter, batter! Home run!

PIONSHIP RIDERS' CUP

HORSE RIDING

I love my horse, Tawny—and I love horse riding! Tawny and I have been riding together since I was a little girl. I love to teach her new things, like trotting and going around barrels. At first Tawny was afraid to do the log jumps. But after lots of practice, we are now champions.

TRACK

I love to run—fast! Relay racing is my favorite track event, because it lets me share my love of running with my friends Nikki and Teresa.

I enjoy lots of sports. They've all taught me how to be a good team member—and to have fun!